Hard Aground

Hard Aground

Rev. Walter Sellars

Breakwater
100 Water Street
P.O. Box 2188
St. John's, NF
A1C 6E6

Canadian Cataloguing in Publication Data

Sellars, Walter.

Hard aground

ISBN 1-55081-014-6

I. Title.

PS8587.E55H37 1992 C813'.54 C92-098560-2
PR9199.3.S45H37 1992

Cover Photo: *Public Archives Canada*

Contents

1

A Mystery Recalled

When a global war erupts, runs its tragic course, and then subsides again into a semblance of peace, it leaves behind, in addition to grief and the monumental task of reconstruction, a whole host of unsung heroes and untold stories. The heroes may be unrecognized because those who witnessed their courage died with them, or because their stories have had to be hidden behind a veil of official secrecy or personal reticence.

One story which came to light a few years ago, quite by accident, revealed that Germany actually had a shore-based weather station, unmanned but serviced by submarines, on the northern tip of the Labrador coast. Parts of that station were recovered and are now stored in our National War Museum in Ottawa.

One hero whose courage involved not only physical bravery but moral determination is the subject of these chapters. He might have been one of war's forgotten heroes if it were not for some people I met in Labrador twenty years after the guns of World War II fell silent.

We now know that the submarine which established and serviced the automatic weather station was not the only one to touch our Canadian shores undetected. There were landings by submarine crews on other parts of the East coast. This is the story of one such landing, but it deals more with compassion and kindness than with hatred and brutality, more with the desire for peace than the urge to make war. The commander of that submarine was a man who had the rare courage to put humanity before official orders.

My name is Ralph Fraser. I was born in Newfoundland and involved with the Canadian forces during World War II in work which might best be described as "intelligence,"— some aspects of which must still remain secret. I can say, however, that my work took me frequently to Goose Bay, that airport built on an almost ideal wilderness plateau providentially placed there when God and nature shaped the world. The construction of that air base in an incredibly short time, beginning in 1941, is a story in itself, vividly told in a book entitled *Checkmate in the North*, by Commander W.G. Carr. From firsthand experience, I can vouch for many of the most interesting details in his book, but the story I am about to tell was hardly even suspected at the time of Commander Carr's death in 1959.

It was 1965 when I took a year away from my own thriving postwar business in Toronto to travel around Labrador and meet its remarkable people. My grandfather had been engaged in summer fishing in Labrador from his own schooner in the early years of this century. His stories had always intrigued me as a boy and, during my own time at Goose Bay during the war, I resolved to return in peacetime and learn more about this harsh land and its kindly people. Subconsciously, perhaps, I was also seeking the answer to a minor mystery which surfaced in 1944 while I was preparing some top secret messages to be sent in cipher to Ottawa and Washington.

In the past few years, the veil of secrecy has been lifted from much of our wartime intelligence activity. We now know about the work of "Intrepid"— Sir William Stephenson— and the unceasing labours of top mathematicians and loyal WRENS (the Women's Royal Naval Service) at Bletchley Park in England, where the most secret messages of the German Armed Forces were unscrambled and made available to Allied generals, admirals and air marshals almost as soon as they were understood by German commanders in the areas of conflict. This cracking of the German cipher was due to our remarkable good fortune in obtaining, even before the war began, a German "Enigma" cipher machine.

My own work often required the use of ciphered messages, and our best machine was known as a TypeX, which was a vast improvement on the Enigma. The TypeX looked like a clumsy electric typewriter, but its output would astonish most office secretaries. By means of a specially inserted hard-fibre disk, about half the size and thickness of a hockey puck, which contained a maze of intricately embedded wires, the TypeX scrambled any message typed into it. The disks were carefully guarded in a safe and frequently changed according to the instructions of a top secret cipher book. When any plain language message was typed into the machine, what appeared on the paper was a series of five-character groups, mixed letters and numbers. This scrambled material was then transmitted by Morse code to its destination where the TypeX process was reversed; typing in the five-letter groups resulted in the automatic recovery of the original message. The Enigma with its five disks was neither as tamper-proof nor as fast as our TypeX, whose secrets were never cracked by the enemy.

In England, certain TypeX machines were modified to help unscramble German Enigma messages, but our Goose Bay machines had no such capability. Therefore, when we intercepted an unusually loud cipher message from a German submarine, we had to send it to England to be unscrambled. This was not so long a process as you might suppose. Goose Bay was a refuelling point for American-made bombers on their way to the conflict, and sometimes scores of them would take off in a single night with Ferry Command pilots at the controls, to refuel again in Iceland and then proceed to Prestwick, Scotland. We could put a courier on one of these planes, and he would be back in three or four days, when bombers fitted for passenger use returned the Ferry

Command crews to Goose Bay for another trans-Atlantic run.

The message which had been intercepted in September 1944 was a report to the commander of the German submarine flotilla operating out of Brest in France. It stated that a certain U-boat (it need not be identified), which had been reported overdue and lost, was actually trapped behind enemy defences and was awaiting the opportunity to escape.

The mystery deepened a few days later when another message, obviously from the same sub, was intercepted giving its position as 53 degrees of north latitude and what appeared to be (through a burst of interference) longitude 61 degrees west. As this would have placed the sub well-inland in Labrador, it was assumed that our operator had misread the one Morse character through the static and that the correct longitude was 51 degrees, putting the sub in the Atlantic well off the Labrador coast.

We had three very efficient direction-finding stations (one in Labrador, one in Newfoundland and one in Nova Scotia) which could get bearings on every submarine within range when they surfaced after dark each day to report to base. We all laughed when two of these stations reported a signal from a sub which appeared to be on dry land. We felt that some freak atmospheric condition had muddled the part of the direction-finding process known as "Sense" and had given bearings 180 degrees removed from the actual. No coastal patrol gasoline or depth charges were wasted on that particular "sighting." The mystery was dismissed as insignificant.

I was back in civilian life for almost twenty years after the war's end before that mystery re-entered my mind. In the meantime I had learned just how much the North Atlantic submarine activity had cost the enemy. It was costly for us, too, of course, and it took brave men to sail in our convoys. But Germany lost almost 28,000 men in submarines, most of them in the Atlantic, and it reached the stage where crews consisted almost exclusively of young men, hardly more than children, hastily trained and sent on missions from which only one out of three submarines ever returned to base. Officially, such forays were never referred to as suicide missions, but Admiral Donitz and his Staff condemned many crews to certain death in the vain hope that some crack in our defences would permit an unexpected attack on a supposedly impregnable position, which would be sufficiently destructive to shake the Allies' increasing certainty of victory.

When I had decided on a year of peacetime Labrador life in the mid 1960s I began to wonder if our phantom submarine was somehow connected with one last desperate attempt to strike at our morale by attacking a previously untouched base right on the North American continent. This was subconsciously on my mind when I set out in 1965 to learn a bit more about the Labrador people than I was able to gather in my brief and busy Goose Bay visits during the war.

To my great satisfaction, the mystery was solved beyond my expectations. I little expected to find at least two other visitors to Labrador who were involved in the same search even more urgently than I was. Our story is told in the next few chapters. I have changed the names of the fine Labrador people who appear as the story unfolds; they may or may not choose to identify themselves later.

My dear wife and two daughters, always ready for adventure, have since spent time with me in Labrador, and they remember the experience and the people with pleasure and affection. On this occasion, they gave me permission to go without them, so they accompanied me to Toronto International Airport (still "Malton" in my Air Force thinking), kissed me good-bye and saw me on the plane for the flight to Montreal, the first leg of my journey. I felt more than a mild thrill of anticipation.

2

Flight North

In 1965, Air Canada had a 4:00 a.m. flight from Montreal to Goose Bay, and I joined the subdued and sleepy passengers who boarded. The profit, if any, was in the great load of freight we carried, for only half the seats were taken. I had been talking to a young girl, a lovely brunette, in the boarding lounge, and the stewardess who obviously had the care of the youngster suggested I should sit with her in a seat just behind the wing where we could look out on two of the four propellers of the turboprop Vanguard.

Thinking it time for an introduction, I said, "I'm Ralph Fraser, age forty-eight."

"And I'm Jenny Matthews, age 15," she replied smiling. "I'm just coming back from visiting my aunt, and this was the first time I've been out of Labrador."

I had gathered as much from our earlier conversation where she had spoken with something akin to wonder of the sights and sounds of Montreal. She reminded me of my own daughters, on that delightful borderline between girl and woman, and totally unaware of her own simple beauty and of the womanly dignity which was vying with her girlish enthusiasm for prominence in a glowing personality.

"I've made the trip many times," I said, "in a single-engined Norseman in 1942 and in DC-3s after that."

"Everybody near Goose Bay has seen those two airplanes," she replied. "When I was very small, I saw lots of planes flying over our village of Otter Creek, but we saw hardly any cars; and I never saw a train until my aunt treated me to a ride from Montreal to Toronto. On my next visit, I've been promised a ride on an old steam train; I've only seen them on television."

Mention of Otter Creek changed the conversation in that direction and, while a smiling stewardess served a most welcome breakfast, I learned that the site of the village was almost overgrown. Its small houses had been home in a humble way to scores of Labrador people doing maintenance work and supplying the unskilled labour which Goose Air Base required. However, being inside the security checkpoint on Department of National Defence property, its people were later uprooted and encouraged to resettle along the Hamilton River where the town of Happy Valley was now home to about 6000 people.

Jenny now felt she knew me well enough to ask the reason for my visit to Labrador and I told her of my wartime connection, my desire to know the people better, and added that I was seeking the answer to some questions which remained when the hostilities ended.

Her reply interested me. She said, "You sound like another visitor named Frank Baird who is boarding at our house. Everybody likes him, but we all wonder why he is here. He boats up the river alone and, asks question about things that happened during the war as though he had some gaps in his memory. He remembers other things very well, according to my mother who lived at Otter Creek then. If you would like to meet Frank, I'll tell him you are my friend."

"Thanks," I said. "Let's shake hands on that bargain and our friendship. Now tell me, how do you get from the airport to Happy Valley?"

There was just a hint of a blush as Jenny answered. "My boyfriend will meet me with his father's car. His name is Ben Carney. Well, he's not exactly my boyfriend, but we have known each other since he took my dolls for rides in his wagon. He is just sixteen and came back from a year in a St. John's school at the end of June. Now he is working at the Hudson's Bay Company and he likes it, but not as well as he likes fishing from his boat in summer and hunting with his Ski-doo in winter. He really doesn't know whether he belongs in a store or in the woods. And he is good in both places; he does everything well."

That last part was spoken with a conviction based on obvious admiration, and I sensed that Ben was a very fortunate young man.

Our approach took us once around the air base. I could see at once that the runways had been lengthened. Four tall antenna masts (I knew them well in 1944) had been removed from their first location and the transmitter huts must have followed them to a new site. I later saw those masts, still in their red and white paint, as shorter lengths of scrap metal in Happy Valley. Circling again as we waited for a Royal Air Force Vulcan to land, I imagined the airport at its wartime busiest. I remembered one winter night when one hundred bombers were checked and refuelled. They then reclaimed the pilots who tumbled out of our Officers' Mess and the crews that were gathered at the hangars, and four hundred engines thundered into life as all the craft cleared the runway in an hour.

Radio silence came into effect immediately after takeoff. There were times when planes and crews came to grief and nobody knew until they were reported overdue in Iceland. Most wrecks were found, some soon, some later. More than once, a trapper found the remains of a crash in the bush or on the Mealy Mountains and drove his dog-team or walked scores of miles to bring the report to the Commanding Officer. Some of those unfortunate planes and crews are yet to be found. I knew that I would be visiting the lonely cemetery to see the stones which marked the final resting place of some of my friends. "They shall not grow old, as we who are left grow old."

We landed without a bump and taxied in to the small terminal. The freshness of the early morning in mid-July was almost a surprise, and the pollution-free air was nothing short of exhilarating. Jenny led me to Ben, who was all eyes and smiles, and introduced him to me with an appealing mixture of shyness and pride. I could see at once why Jenny spoke of him with such warmth; here was a young man who could look the whole world in the face, to quote Longfellow. Ben's handshake was firm and friendly; I really meant it when I said, "I'm very glad to meet you."

Our baggage was not long in being offloaded and claimed. I gladly accepted Ben's offer to take me to the home of my host, a longtime friend who worked for the Department of Transport and who lived in one of the comfortable houses that the government provided. Jenny, with a smile, told Ben that I was another wanderer like Frank Baird, and that brought an immediate response.

"Frank and I were up the river again in my boat on Saturday," said Ben, "and when we got to Tumbledown Brook, he asked if we could circle around while he looked along both shores through his binoculars. Then we coasted along for a while at trolling speed, went ashore to boil the kettle and have a good meal, and lay on a smooth rock soaking up the sun and talking. He seemed suddenly happy, and on the way home, he told me he was beginning to remember things he had forgotten for twenty years. When we got back to the valley, I dropped him off at your house and your mother later told me that he was asking questions about things that happened in 1944."

"What sort of things?" asked Jenny.

Ben's reply made me sit bolt upright in the back seat. "He wanted to know if any of the Labrador trappers ever found strangers along their traplines during the war. He wondered if any food disappeared from their tilts or tents, and he seemed to know as well as we do that no trapper would ever steal from another. He seemed especially anxious to know if anybody ever met men wearing any other uniform than that of a Canadian soldier or airman, or a Newfoundland Ranger."

"What a strange question," said Jenny, and their conversation turned briefly to the interests of young people nearly, or perhaps head over heels, in love.

As for me, I had just heard of a man asking a question which had been buried in my subconscious for more than twenty years. Now I knew that my visit to Labrador was not merely to write my own social history of the natives and liveyers. Now I knew that Frank Baird and I, if he was willing, would be putting our heads together for a very earnest talk indeed.

3

Returning Memory

Frank and I arranged to meet in the RCAF Officers' Mess, where we had both been granted honorary memberships because of wartime service on the base. We compared notes and decided that we really had not met during the war, probably because both of us were in and out of Goose Air Base at irregular intervals.

"My work was really in the engineering side of radio equipment for combat aircraft," he said, "but I flew the Atlantic a dozen times with Ferry Command in two-engined B-25s or four-engined B-17s acting as wireless operator while I checked the performance of various equipment modifications. There was not a lot to do except at takeoff and approach, but we kept a listening-watch all the way across in case we could intercept signals from enemy submarines and give a debriefing report on their probable location. Even their surface speed with diesel power would not let them travel very far in an hour or two, and their speed when submerged was very slow when running under electric power at low revolutions to conserve battery capacity. I think we were responsible for a couple of successful depth charge attacks, but from what I've since learned about Admiral Donitz's submarine fleet in 1944, I can't help feeling sorry for the poor young fellows trapped helplessly two hundred feet below with the battered pressure hull springing a new leak with every sea-splitting charge our coastal command dropped. The submarine service must be the most gut-wrenching of all combat duties."

Why did I have the feeling that Frank's sympathy for submariners had something very personal about it? His gaze had shifted from me and he was staring into space over my shoulder as if he were trying to bring something vague, but very important, into sharper focus.

Suddenly he reached into his pocket and produced a white scarf much like the ones we Air Force officers wore when stepping out in our greatcoats. He held it up and showed the initials *EMR* neatly embroidered near one end. "To get back to my story," he said, "if I could ever find out who originally owned this scarf, I feel I would rest much easier. I may very well owe my life to the man who wore it, and there were gaps in my memory, or perhaps my consciousness, which compelled me to return to Labrador in what is probably a hopeless attempt to give the scarf back to its owner or his family. My returning here has brought missing details to the surface of my mind, and now I can recall most of what happened."

Reducing Frank's story to narrative form, it appears that his plane was one of the twenty-five Mitchell B-25s which took off from Goose Air Base on the night of October 3, 1944. There were only four on board: the pilot, the co-pilot, a navigator named Johnny Webber, and Frank. They had hardly cleared the runway when one engine lost power. The pilot gave them a warning over the intercom and said he would try for more height so that he could turn back. But with the wheels still down and the other engine spluttering, it was hopeless and, with hardly a thousand feet of altitude, he shouted that the others could bail out or stick with him. The truth is, there was not much of a choice; a thousand feet is not enough altitude to clear the escape hatch and get a parachute opened.

The end came quickly. Somewhere up the Hamilton River from the Base, the plane completed its turn toward the distant runway, but it crashed just in from the shore, both wings torn off by the impact with the tall evergreens, and the fuselage splitting open in a narrow, swampy clearing.

Frank was the only survivor. He remembers the horrible tearing sound of wrenched and tortured metal, and then all was black oblivion.

It was daylight when consciousness returned. He was lying on a bed of evergreen boughs, one eye swollen almost shut, pains shooting through his arms and back, and his right leg broken but carefully and almost expertly braced with two small evergreen trunks as splints and with the initialled scarf and strips torn from his own and somebody else's clothing holding the splints in place. Leaning over him was an unshaven but most welcome face which introduced itself in lilting Labrador speech as Charlie Crowley, "the

Ancient of Days but still a trapper." A tin kettle sat over a nearby fire, and Charlie was offering Frank tea from a tin mug.

Frank was glad to accept, and glad also of the thick slice of bread, made delicious by his hunger and by the molasses and raisins which flavoured it. "Trapper's bread," said Charlie. "My woman— that's my wife in your way of speaking— makes it like nobody else. It's a little bit of home when I'm lonely on my trapline."

"What about the others in my crew?" asked Frank.

"Sorry, my boy," said Charlie quietly, "there was nothing I could do for them. And now, if you will promise not to try anything foolish like moving around, I'll leave you with the rest of this kettle of tea, and some bread, and I'll be off to Goose Bay by my boat and overland to get help."

Frank had no desire to move. With pain attacking every square inch of his body, he lapsed in and out of consciousness and sleep until the Norseman rescue plane swooped overhead and landed on its floats to disgorge the medical officer and two orderlies with a stretcher. Then came Charlie's boat again with a small crew of crash-experienced personnel. Frank remembered feeling grateful that neither of the inevitable body bags was for him, and then the anaesthetic took hold. He woke up in hospital and smiled thankfully at a young nursing sister who looked nothing short of beautiful as she gently adjusted his pillows.

"Now," said Frank as we prepared to eat lunch with officers who seemed young, but were actually no younger than I was in 1944, "here is the mystery. I was dimly conscious several times as my broken leg was set and splinted. There were at least three men around me. One of them spoke to me in good English, but he spoke almost in whispers to the others in words that I could not catch. I believe these were in some other language. Old Charlie saw them as he came up the river in his outboard. He had spotted the wreck when his quick eyes noticed the splintered treetops but, by the time he landed, the strangers had reached the edge of the bush and shouted that they had work to do upstream. One of them stayed in sight long enough to ask Charlie if he could arrange a rescue, and then he also disappeared. I was already splinted and bedded down when Charlie arrived."

"Couldn't he describe the men?" I asked. Frank shook his head. "He knew they were not Labrador people, and they were not members of the Newfoundland Rangers. You know that they patrolled Labrador before Newfoundland joined Confederation; they became Mounties then and gave up their Ranger khaki for RMCP uniforms. In any case, there was only one Ranger stationed at Goose Bay. All Charlie could tell me is that they appeared to be wearing jackets much like the heavy blue watch-jackets worn by the men of the Canadian Navy vessels which were often in Terrington Basin at Goose Bay. The one who asked Charlie to go for help seemed to be wearing a peaked cap with a white crown."

Frank then went on to say that, with a cast replacing the splint, he asked to be taken to the crash site a week later. Not much had been cleared away. The most pathetic thing about it was a parachute wrapped around the starboard propeller.

"Johnny Webber must have got out of the forward escape hatch," said Frank. "He was keen on photography and he was up in the nose, in the bomb-aimer's position, taking dramatic movies of takeoff and low-level flight. He must have pulled the rip cord as soon as he wriggled out, and the whirling prop wound his chute up, shrouds and all, till it killed him. I cut off a piece of that parachute and I keep it as something almost sacred.

"Nobody at the base paid too much attention to my story of the men who picked me out of the wreck or the swamp and splinted my leg. The medical officer said they certainly saved my life. But he also said I was probably delirious for hours and would have been confused even without the bump over my eye. They may have been airmen from the base doing a little questionable poaching, or trappers that Charlie did not recognize from a distance.

"I kept in touch with Charlie till he died about five years ago. He swore to the last that my rescuers did not belong to Labrador. And there is still the scarf. The initials did not belong to anybody in the neighbourhood, nor to anybody on the base. The warrant officer in charge of the orderly room checked every name on the Station roll call and no initials coincided with *EMR*.

"So there's the mystery," said Frank, "but I have discovered that there is somebody else presently at the base, a young meteorological man by the name of Karl Runsted, who has been exploring the river in a rented boat as I was doing with Ben Carney, asking questions about how the sandbars change at different seasons, and other questions about navigation in Lake Melville and on the river. Let's get to know him."

4

Interlude

Two days later, a Wednesday, Frank telephoned to say that he had spoken to Karl Runsted and had set up a meeting with him for the following Tuesday. Karl seemed a bit reluctant, and Frank felt that the delay in the appointment was Karl's way of gaining time to think through this sudden interest on the part of strangers.

I was almost relieved at the delay because my host, Pete Humphries, had dropped a couple of comments which I found interesting. We were in a Department of Transport transmitter building and Pete had just shown me a massive RCA transmitter into which you could actually walk through a switch-protected door to examine the barrel-sized low-frequency coils and tub-sized capacitors.

"It's an old-timer," said Pete. "I tuned it on frequency a good many times when I was an Air Force sergeant during the war. Many people considered Goose Bay to be the Siberia of all postings, but I enjoyed it and that is why I'm spending my last years before retirement in Labrador again. This old rig used to sit up on the plateau where the base is located, in one of three main huts several miles from the hangars and all the messes and living quarters. The huts were spaced out for obvious wartime reasons, though we ordinary joes honestly did not expect an attack.

"Nevertheless, there were several funny things which we never did explain. About six of us, stationed in the transmitter area, had our own bunks in one of the huts known affectionately as 'Dew Drop Inn'. The transmitters were operated by remote control from the base itself, but the tuning and maintenance had to be done on the spot, and

31

the furnaces needed round the clock fuelling. We ran our own show, cooked our own meals, and those of us who could stand the isolation wouldn't change places with anybody; we could always call for transport back to the base if half of us wanted to attend a USO show or some other entertainment. We even had one sergeant who could bake a fine chocolate cake by using a covered roasting pan as an oven and poking the whole thing into the fire pot of the big wood-fired furnace.

"In September of 1944, when we decided to bring our canned rations indoors from the unheated shed, we found that some of the cartons were empty. We really did not have to account for the rations, so we just shrugged it off, even though we were puzzled since our rare visitors came from the base in a jeep or a four-by-four and left as soon as their business was done. They never got near our supplies, so we knew they were not the thieves.

"Then another unusual thing happened. We were armed, in a manner of speaking, with old Ross rifles which just sat in the rack. There came a day when we were ordered to dump or turn in our old ammunition so, for a few days, we had the sport of trying to clip branches off distant trees over the edge of the plateau down toward the Hamilton River. Well, on one clear, still day when sound travelled for miles, our barrage of bullets seemed to stir up all hell down in the valley. For just a couple of minutes there were startled shouts, and I'll be blessed if I could understand what was being said. We stopped firing, and shrugged again.

"One evening, a couple of our men attending a USO show sat next to a civilian labourer whose home was in a small fishing community on the coast well south of Cartwright. He casually said that his neighbours had seen a German submarine close inshore and had even talked to a landing party. However, since the man said that the matter had been reported to the nearest Ranger, we felt that things were taken care of, and as you know, the army men stationed at Goose Bay never had to fire a shot in anger. Boredom was their main enemy as they manned their artillery and anti-aircraft guns."

Pete obviously considered the matter closed, but his comments sent me out to the coast despite the twenty years that had elapsed. A civilian with a Piper Cub flew me to Cartwright where I caught up with the MS *Nonia* on her way south. Older crew-members had heard of sub sightings when they serviced the coastal communities from the old SS *Kyle* during the war, but they had been unmolested.

When the *Nonia* dropped me into a small boat to go ashore at Minnie's Brook (not its real name because it is so small and I have no desire to subject the people to unwanted publicity), I found hospitable if plain shelter and food with the family of Jed Manuel. Jed took me to see Steve Wilcox, and Steve was adamant that he and another man, now dead, had seen an inflateable boat, obviously launched from a larger vessel that was not visible, come around a headland into a cove where they actually helped the three men make a clumsy landing on the rocks. Only one man spoke with them, and that was politely and in good English. The questions had more to do with life on the coast than with military secrets; it was probably just a probe to see if the coast could be approached.

When pressed to name the year, Steve decided on late 1940, too early to have much to do with my search. The submarine was not seen on this occasion and Steve was a bit apologetic about being casual at the time, though the news did get to the Ranger eventually.

"You see, sir," he said, "we knew there was a war on, but it didn't affect our lives very much. Sometimes our battery radio worked and sometimes it didn't. We had hardly any news. Things weren't much different along the coast in 1940 than they were in the first war. That ended in November, 1918, but we didn't know it was over until January of 1919— and then only because two veterans from up around Mud Lake on Hamilton Inlet were walking home. They had gotten as far as St. Anthony after their discharge and there was no shipping further north in December. So they somehow got across the strait to the Labrador coast by small boat and on the ice, and then walked the rest of the way, about three hundred miles, though one of them had been wounded in the leg. We bunked them and fed them for a day or two, gave them a bit of grub, fixed up their snowshoes, and on they went in spite of a near-blizzard. You can still talk to one of them in Happy Valley. They passed through here in January and got home sometime in February. There were no radios then, so they were the ones who brought the news that the war was over. We weren't quite that shut off from the world in 1940, but we wouldn't have known the enemy just by talking to them."

Well, I wasn't much further along in my search, except for meeting other people who were convinced that submarines could easily approach the coast, but I was glad of a couple of days with some kind and dignified people, who made a living on a bleak coast which most of us would shun, but to which they clung with tenacity and real affection.

One story touched me. It had to do with the problem of education in isolated communities.

Jed brought up the subject with a touch of sadness and some indignation, but mostly with resignation.

"We'd like our children to have more schooling," he said. "Most of the grown-ups here can't read or write. About four winters ago, six of the men went inland to hunt for deer because their families at home were hungry. They arrived at a big tilt, a rough-and-ready cabin used by any hunter or trapper on the trail, after several days of travel. They had no luck at all and came home dog-tired with no fresh meat. But one man brought back a note which hunters from further up the coast had pinned to the wall of the tilt, but he didn't think of giving it to John Hibbs to read until weeks later. The note said:

'One mile to the northwest we have left four frozen deer which we killed for you people of Minnie's Brook.'

"Not one of the six hunters could read the note when they found it, so the caribou thawed and rotted in the marsh while the families went hungry."

There was silence in Jed's small kitchen only interrupted by his wife's kind invitation to have another cup of tea. I had learned more than I expected about the harshness of life on the Labrador coast, where even toothache was a major scourge, there being only one dentist for fifteen thousand scattered people.

Good fortune brought calm weather on Tuesday, and the Piper Cub came all the way to Minnie's Brook, made a perfect landing on pontoons that looked too big for it and took me back to Goose Bay, landing with hardly a splash on the river at Happy Valley, just behind the new hospital, in the late morning of a glorious sunny day.

Entering the drugstore, Happy Valley's newest business, I had time to phone the Officers' Mess to see if we could bring a civilian in for an evening, and I was generously offered a private corner where Frank and I could talk with Karl Runsted. Suddenly, I sensed the excitement of anticipation and I felt impatient for evening to come, but I could not foresee just how far that young meteorologist would take us on our search.

5

Progress

Coming out of the drugstore after my telephone call, I met Jenny and was warmly invited to have lunch at her house. "Won't that put your mother to a lot of trouble?" I asked. Laughing, she shook her head.

"Mom's used to people dropping in," she said. "She baked bread this morning and was rather disappointed that Mr. Baird would not be there to judge it. You can have his share, and you can meet Ben again because I've invited him as well."

I was sorry for Frank's absence, but glad of a chance to talk with Ben, who came in with "Here I am" in lieu of a knock— nothing strange in Labrador. My first good impression of him was strengthened as he greeted Mrs. Matthews with a son-like hug and put his arm briefly around Jenny's waist affectionately but more self-consciously. His greeting to me was accompanied by his firm handshake.

Mrs. Matthews was an older Jenny, gracious, unaffected, just as lovely— and younger than I imagined. "She's ten years younger than I am," was my first thought, "and just might have been one of the bright youngsters I danced with at special civilian entertainments during the war."

My musing was·interrupted by her smiling apology for her husband's absence. "He is a surveyor and is miles upstream surveying the river to assess the impact of the dam at Churchill Falls," she said. "They even want us to use the name Churchill for the river, but it will always be the Grand to the real old-timers and the Hamilton to the rest of us. We object to having the government change the name without even a by-your-leave to the people who own and use it; but the river will freeze and thaw and move its sand around the same as it always did, whatever they call it." And she invited us to a table where the fresh bread was almost outdone by the soup and dumplings. At her invitation, I tried molasses as s spread on my bread. "It's the fancy grade," she said, "though even the black-strap tasted good to me as a child when sweet treats and candy were scarce and an orange in the toe of a stocking at Christmas was a treasure almost too rare to eat."

This was spoken not with complaint, but matter-of-factly as I have many times heard Labrador people speak of great hardship and near-tragedy.

Lunch being over, Ben had some interesting news before returning to the Hudson's Bay store. "Jenny went up the river with me on Saturday," he said, "because I was curious about the way Mr. Baird acted the last time we were there. I beached the boat on the sand about where Mr. Baird had been focusing his binoculars, and we walked around in the swampy ground with our shoes off. Jenny spotted the bent blade of an airplane propeller sticking out of the grass, and I believe there is a whole engine sunk in the mud. I know where the remains of two other airplanes are, one of them underwater off John Groves' Point, but I don't think many people remember this one.

Do you think Mr. Baird knows something about it?"

"You should ask him," I replied, realizing that Frank would now have confirmation that he had rightly identified the crash site. "Frank will have quite a story to tell later, and we may have a use for your boat if you and Jenny can taxi us around on your days off in the next few weeks." Anticipation of adventure showed in Ben's quick smile as he waved to all and allowed Jenny to accompany him to the door.

Thanking Mrs. Matthews for her genuine hospitality, I asked her to advise Frank that our evening meeting with Karl would be at the Mess. I then headed to Pete's place by one of the Valley's many taxis for a shave and a change of duds. Pete's wife was "outside," meaning not in Labrador, having gone for a visit to her native Winnipeg, so Pete made dinner. Then we played the opening round of a game of chess before Frank arrived to accompany me to the base.

The bar steward pointed Karl out to us when Frank and I got to the Mess. He was a tall, intelligent-looking young man tending toward blonde, polite and well-spoken, but perhaps a bit on his guard as he met with two strangers whose curiosity he couldn't understand. From the brief biography he offered, I put his age at twenty-five, since he said he had come to Canada with his parents in 1950, from Wuppertal "near Dusseldorf" in Germany when he was ten years old.

He knew we were curious about his interest in the Hamilton River, and it took us only a few minutes to assure him that ours was not an official inquiry into his wanderings. When he knew that we were also involved in a quest, he began to see us as allies, and we soon discovered that his request for a meteorological posting to Goose Bay had little to do with any unique features of Labrador weather and a lot to do with his own ancestry.

"I'm here because of my grandfather," he said, and the story began to unfold as Frank and I sat almost spellbound. Uniformed officers came and went. RAF men who had just flown the Atlantic in Vulcans greeted Canadian fliers who had just returned from exercises with the Americans who had their own Mess on the other side of the base. The padre and the medical officer, who knew that Frank and I were leftovers from World War II, greeted us with a smile and a wave and moved on. Conversations and hail-fellow laughter were heard, but not really heard, as young Karl told his story. Frank was as still as the Sphinx and almost as breathless.

"My grandfather was one of the oldest submarine commanders during the war," said

Karl. "My father was a corporal in the army, and neither he nor my grandmother had any idea of the ghastly loss of life in the submarine service. Nobody will ever know the real fate of hundreds of lost crews, so although my grandfather is officially listed as 'missing in action, presumed dead,' we are grateful that we know something of his last days. I am in Labrador to follow up some leads which we gathered from one member of his crew, and my father and mother live in Toronto where they have traced the only other crewmember we know of, but he is not yet willing to tell all he knows.

"Apparently my grandfather was dispatched on what could only be called a terror mission when a German victory was seen as utterly hopeless by all but the fanatics. He was given a young crew, only half the usual number of torpedoes, more than usual ammunition for his deck gun and the anti-aircraft guns, and enough stores for months at sea, or under it. His job was to cruise up and down the northeastern coast of Newfoundland and the coast of Labrador, sinking coastal steamers by torpedoes while they lasted, and then firing on small boats and undefended coastal villages in what could only be described as slaughter for the sake of revenge. His last task, probably of the suicide class, was to get into Hamilton Inlet, up Lake Melville into Terrington Basin, and do all the damage he could to storage tanks, hangars, aircraft and personnel. He and his crew were considered expendable.

"We learned none of this from official records, but only from the one crewmember who got back home. Apparently my grandfather was a great admirer of Martin Niemoller, a submarine hero in World War I who became a clergyman and was imprisoned and tortured by the Nazis for his stubborn opposition to World War II. Incidentally, Niemoller survived his torture and even visited Canada about the time I was born. Anyhow, my grandfather had been sickened by reports of the 1942 torpedoing of the SS *Caribou* on its regular run between North Sydney and Port aux Basques with the loss of 132 innocent lives, and now, about August of 1944, he made a pact with his young crew that they would attack none but armed naval vessels.

"They did get into Lake Melville and they were seen, but apparently the aircraft which spotted them was not armed. They submerged and later felt depth charges exploding at a distance and almost ran out of fuel. They could not make radio contact with one of the 'sea cows' as the underwater tankers were called, and if you know anything about submarines you will know that they can't navigate underwater forever without a battery recharge.

"So my grandfather decided to ascend Hamilton River, find some secluded spot, and wait till he could make a rendezvous with a sea cow. To give you just an outline of the rest, the German submarine pens along the French coast were under constant attack, communications were disorganized, and his orders seemed to tell him to get most of his crew to the coast (where landings and pickups were more frequent than Canada realized) and keep two engineers and the navigator with him in case a breakout was possible. The crew stole a motorboat somewhere, got to the coast and were picked up by a home-bound sub which had spent all its torpedoes.

"That sub never got home. It was spotted on the surface by a Canso aircraft and was depth-charged as it submerged. Submarine training outlined a slow and clumsy underwater escape procedure; one man got out, a member of my grandfather's crew. He was picked up by a corvette, spent the rest of the war in a POW camp near Peterborough, and told the story to my grandmother and my father after his repatriation.

"We still don't know my grandfather's fate. We know he had tried to get back down the Hamilton River, but was frustrated by changing sandbars which made the water too shallow even after he got rid of his deck guns and all possible weight. I believe his submarine is still somewhere in the river. When I first came here I spotted what looked like a toppled conning tower at the entrance of the creek leading to Mud Lake, but it turned out to be a couple of rusty boilers from an old tug that had once rafted logs for a long-dead lumber company."

There was silence for a moment in our corner of the lounge. Then Frank came out of a near trance and asked quietly, "What was your grandfather's name?"

"Ernest Runsted," said Karl.

"Did he have a middle name?"

"Yes," replied Karl, "it was Martin."

Frank reached into his jacket pocket and retrieved something which he held out to Karl. "You can see the initials," he said. "This is your grandfather's scarf. I would like to join you in your search for a very honourable officer and gentleman."

Karl touched the scarf in a stunned and reverent silence, and then I was witness to an emotional handshake and a silent pact sealed with the eyes.

6

Narrowing the Gap

With Pete's wife away in Winnipeg visiting her parents, we sat up late that evening over our chess game, neither of us playing at our best because conversation was as important as a checkmate. I told Pete the story which Karl had shared with Frank and myself.

Pete absorbed it quietly, pondered it through the next five or six moves, and then said, "I believe that sub was sighted in the river in 1944."

Trying to be as cool as he was, I lost a bishop through a move which had too little of my attention. Pete correctly interpreted my loss of concentration as an indication of impatient curiosity.

"Nowadays," he said, removing the bishop and threatening my queen, "a submarine could never get past Happy Valley without being spotted by somebody. But it was not like that in 1944 when our Labrador employees were mostly resident in Otter Creek. So, running on its electric motors rather than diesel, and navigating after dark with its depth sounders finding the deeper channels around the sandbars, a sub might remain undetected by the few people who lived or camped close to the shore. The sandbars themselves pose very little threat to a sub's hull; local people often run aground and then back off unharmed unless they are travelling at speed just after the ice moves out about the third week of May. Then the bars are frozen as solid as concrete.

"But I should introduce you to old Wallace Swyers. He worked for the McNamara Company when the base was under construction and was kept on as a maintenance foreman. One day, he was supervising a small job near Dew Drop Inn, where we needed to bury a lot of long copper wires as a counterpoise to our main antenna; that sort of thing is necessary when the antenna sits above dry, sandy soil. Well, Wallace said he was camping on Birch Island on weekends, and one night, he heard a humming sound closer than the base, which was about six miles away. Looking out over the river he thought he saw a bulky, ghostly shape moving upstream near the further shore, but the night was so dark that it was a case of black against black. The matter only came up because we had been talking about local superstitions and apparitions, and it stuck in my mind only because of the voices we heard when we were wasting our old ammunition a few weeks before."

"However," said Pete, wincing as he lost a rook to my knight, "putting that memory alongside what Karl told you this evening, I think you should look for your submarine upstream from Happy Valley. Besides, the Mud Lake men have always fished for trout and salmon lower down the river and out along the lake shore, and nothing as large as a sub could stay hidden there for twenty years."

Looking for Ben at the Hudson's Bay Company next morning, I was surprised to see two men carrying a casket out of the storehouse. Ben laughed at my puzzled look.

"It's not a secret burial," he said. "We stock caskets because there is no funeral director in Happy Valley. Family members or friends prepare the body for burial and we sell the caskets at sixty-five dollars, just above cost. This one is going to the hospital where a very old gentleman died before dawn."

In answer to my request for a boat trip upriver on Saturday, Ben eagerly agreed. "Let's make a proper picnic of it," he said. "Will it be okay if Jenny goes with us?"

And so we went— Karl, Frank, Jenny, Ben and myself. Ben's boat was a sensible cedar-strip craft of adequate size and looking more businesslike than the newer fibreglass or plastic models which still seemed experimental and brittle by comparison. The eighteen horsepower outboard motor would be scorned by many of today's youth, but Ben's interest was more in the wild beauty around him than in senseless speed.

Only once or twice did we run at full throttle because we poked in and out along both shores scanning every possible place where a submarine could hide. Don't forget that with its ballast tanks fully flooded, it could rest on a fairly deep bottom with only a fraction of the superstructure showing. We arrived at Tumbledown Brook, where a busy stream came over smooth rocks and into the Hamilton, just about noon. The sun was bright and the day glorious.

Jenny was as nimble as Ben, but twice as graceful, as she helped him beach the boat. She arranged a few large stones in a fireplace circle while Ben gathered dry wood for a fire. Only those of you who have eaten outdoors in unspoiled surroundings can imagine the smell of the woodsmoke, the gourmet quality of beans and bacon stirred together in an open frying pan, the taste of tea from an old veteran of a tin kettle much blackened by use, and the sense of well-being which makes you wish that you could capture the moment forever. We finished our last slice of homemade bread while Karl, Frank and I voted Jenny and Ben the best chefs in the world.

Then Jenny went to the boat and returned with a box she had brought aboard with unusual care. A hint of mischief made her smile even livelier as she sat down again and opened the box to reveal a perfect cake which said, "Happy Birthday, Ben." No seventeen-year-old boy could possibly look happier, though a mite taken aback. But only for a moment. The cake had to wait while he reached into an inside pocket of his jacket and produced a small velvet jewel case.

"You caught me by surprise," he said, "so you'll have to accept your birthday gift three weeks early. I've been carrying it with me everywhere since it arrived by mail order a month ago." He produced a delicate gold chain, from which hung a beautifully crafted caged pearl.

We three witnesses applauded, and Jenny got up so that Ben could stand behind her to clasp the chain around her neck. Then there was the briefest hug and kiss, but a longer one could not have expressed more affection and tenderness. As we shared the cake with much good-natured bantering, I thought to myself, "When those young people finally make a commitment to each other, there will be no nonsense about it. It will be heartfelt and it will be forever."

Frank must have read my thoughts. As he and I strolled up the sloping rock to examine a vein of mineral where the brook chuckled over a low, stone ledge, he said, "What parents would not be proud of such youngsters? I've been living at Jenny's house for a month and I've only once seen her cheerfulness dampened. She is a volunteer aide at the hospital, helping with the play program in the children's ward. She was especially fond of a frail Eskimo child from further north, a two-year-old girl who understood no English but whose face lit up whenever Jenny came to share a simple game with her. The child had an endearing habit of going through the motions of pat-a-cake if she thought she had failed or had displeased a grown-up in any way.

"Jenny arrived at the hospital one afternoon to learn that the child was near death, and when Jenny joined the two caring nurses at the bedside, the little girl, as if to apologize for being a bother, brought her small hands together once or twice in the pat-a-cake manner, looked appealingly into Jenny's eyes, and then closed her own eyes for the last time.

"It took a while for Jenny to recover her good spirits after a loss so personal but, with Ben's understanding sympathy, she won through after she and Ben went back to the grave a day or two after the actual burial and placed there a small wooden cross which Ben had made. Those two young people are made of good stuff," Frank added as we came back to join the others.

Sitting or lying on the smooth rocks, we basked in the sun for a half hour before taking to the water again. Then we proceeded a bit upstream and across to the other side to explore, by mutual agreement, the swampy clearing which Ben and Jenny had visited the previous week and where Frank and his friends had come to grief a full two decades previously.

The other three of us respected the quietness of Frank and Karl as they stepped ashore first. I remembered that Ben and Jenny had explored the swampy soil barefoot, and as we all prepared to do the same, I recalled some words which Moses had heard so long ago, "Take your shoes from off your feet, for the place whereon you tread is holy ground." It certainly seemed that way to Karl, the closest he had ever come to his grandfather; and it was a place of great meaning to Frank whose life had here hung in the balance while his three companions were beyond the help which unexpected rescuers could offer.

Ben led us to the place where he and Jenny had found the bent tip of a propeller and Frank said, "I wish I had brought a shovel."

"If you are thinking about digging," said Ben, "we could move this soft soil with a paddle and our hands." He ran to the boat and returned with the paddle. We took turns digging, just keeping ahead of the water which seeped into our excavation, until Frank was able to reach into the shallow hole and touch the hub of the propeller. We wondered what he was up to until he finally withdrew his hand, and with it, the ends of some mud-soaked but still intact nylon cords.

"The shrouds of poor Johnny Webber's parachute," he said. "This is where my three friends died and where I would have died if it had not been for an enemy who put humanity before so-called patriotic duty. You told me, Karl, that your grandfather had worked for a time in England in the 1930s, so he must have been the one who spoke good English to me and who turned back from the edge of the woods over there to make sure that Charlie Crowley could get word to the base. Your grandfather and his men seemed to be headed inland at that point, so we have no way of knowing whether their hideout was upstream or down. But I'm all for going a bit further upstream before calling it a day."

Three of us turned back to the boat, leaving Frank standing at the crash site with his arm around Karl's shoulder. It was a moment on which none of us wished to intrude, and we busied ourselves with putting on our socks and shoes until Frank and Karl joined us.

The rest of the afternoon was uneventful except for the opportunity to wonder at the untapped timber resources along the riverbanks. There were hundreds of thousands of acres in which the sound of an axe had never been heard; only in a country like Canada, where we averaged six or seven people per square mile, could such natural wealth remain untouched. Sooner or later, we would have to do what Finland was doing in a latitude equally handicapped by a restricted navigation season, and put a well-planned environmentally compatible paper mill on the very doorstep of the raw materials. We could see that trees came to maturity and toppled from old age without doing anything more than enriching an already rich soil. Our search for the elusive submarine had been unsuccessful, but in every other way the day had yielded rich dividends. We returned home more refreshed than tired after a day of real companionship. I was no sooner out of the shower at Pete's house than Pete called me to the telephone.

An excited Karl informed me that he had had a long-distance call from his father in Toronto. "The other crewmember, Werner Holtz had given my father his diaries and other records," he said. "Werner's health is not good enough for any strenuous trip and a personal visit to the river. But I believe his information tells us where we must look next. Could you arrange for an airplane to take us on an air search tomorrow?"

7

The Sighting

*P*ete managed on short notice to charter a
Beaver aircraft for Sunday afternoon. The
Beaver was a superb successor to the
Norseman in which I had flown for many hours
and, by 1965, there were about 1600 Beavers
in service throughtout the world. Today, the
pilot had agreed to buzz Happy Valley before
landing on the river, to let us know when he

would be back from a morning flight to Cartwright. Frank was staying at the Matthews home, and Karl and I were also to be lunch guests of Mrs. Matthews when she, Jenny and Ben returned from church.

We counted heads and decided there was room in the Beaver for Pete as well, so Mrs. Matthews put another plate on the table and had me telephone a willing Pete, who was still fending for himself in his wife's absence, to invite him to lunch with the rest of us. I was getting used to Labrador hospitality, a refreshing change from the coldness of urban life.

As we ate, Karl filled us in on the phone call from his father. "Dad only gave me a few details about the submarine's probable location," he said. "He will put the rest of the information in a letter. Werner knows nothing of place names, of course, but according to his description the submarine must be at Muskrat Falls."

"Well, it certainly couldn't be further up," said Ben. "I've been going to the Falls all my life and have been there a dozen times since I got my own boat two years ago. A first glance will tell you that absolutely no boat could navigate those rapids. Lots of people still go there regularly and some of them portage their canoes along the bank to reach smoother water again further up. Nobody has seen anything as large as a sub. Is it possible it was scuttled in the deep water under the Falls?"

"I've been there only once," said Karl. "I noticed the turbulence and I followed another boat which skirted the rough water by making a big circle to the left. Do most people take that precaution?"

"Yes," replied Ben. "Hardly anybody takes the risk of making a beeline across the turbulence. A small boat might easily be tugged to the centre and sucked under if its motor failed. Most times there is a very swift whirlpool, and I've seen large logs and other debris sucked under without ever coming to the surface again, unless they are spun out somewhere along the edge of the pool. I once pushed off from the shore at what I thought was a safe distance from the current; my motor needed three or four pulls before it started, and I was surprised, and even scared, at how quickly the boat was grabbed and pulled toward the centre."

"Would a more powerful craft have a better chance in the turbulence?" was my question. "I've seen the *Maid of the Mist* go fairly close to Niagara Falls."

"That's my question, too," said Karl, "because Werner told my father that the helmsman turned to starboard when they hit the turbulence."

Ben jumped up and paced the floor in excitement. "That's something I hadn't thought of," and his face was animated and eager. "I don't know of any average boat going around to the right, but if there was a small cove there with high banks and lots of trees, a large craft might just remain hidden. I think all the portaging is done to the left of the whirlpool so there's almost no reason for a trapper to go along the other side."

Now all of us were excited. Karl added, "You might think the sub would be seen from the air, but all of us at the base know that, at that point, most aircraft are low after takeoff or during approach and the ground goes by pretty fast. Also, Werner said they flooded some tanks till they hit the bottom and then dismantled the projecting sections of both periscopes. They also cut scores of trees and laid them against the hull and conning tower, so what we have to look for is a lot of dead trees in some sort of a manmade pattern. If they were on the ground they'd have rotted by now, but sitting high and dry, they'd probably just lose their bark and stay sound for decades."

We were just finishing lunch when the Beaver swooped overhead, circled low and dipped to the river. Mrs. Matthews smilingly cut short our thanks by saying, "Be off with you. There's work to be done."

On the way to the river, I made a suggestion in the interests of present secrecy. "Let's keep the purpose of our search from the pilot," I said. "He must be used to flying tourists and dignitaries around the Falls, so Frank and I can be the tourists. Ben can sit in the co-pilot's seat and advise the pilot where to fly, at what altitude, and when to circle, and we can all keep our eyes open for the sub. We can ask for about five thousand feet of altitude to begin with, and I'll let my camera be obvious so as to give an excuse for several passes back and forth. It we're lucky an hour in the air should do it, and we can signal Ben to have the pilot turn for home when we've seen what we want."

The flight was almost an anticlimax. We thoroughly enjoyed it, of course. The Beaver is not as nimble as the wartime Harvard, a low-wing beauty much loved by pilots in training, but people who have done all their flying in 747s or other aircraft almost as big should sometimes try the altogether different sensation of flying with just a few friends in a Beaver or an Otter.

In about ten minutes, we reached the Falls, really a series of spectacular rapids but with the capacity of generating a few million watts of electrical power if their beauty is ever destroyed for the sake of utility. We circled a few times at several altitudes until Frank pointed out the starboard windows at dead trees in a definite pattern and, barely visible, the unmistakable shape of a conning tower. On the next sweep, Ben had the pilot bank the Beaver the other way so that Jennie and Karl could see what Frank, Pete and I had already seen.

Then we had the pilot fly around for a bit of diversionary sightseeing, with a pass over the base itself after permission from the tower on a corner of a hangar, and we finally made a perfect landing just downstream from Birch Island. After our formal thanks, Jenny took time to thank the pilot more warmly for a thoroughly enjoyable hour aloft, and we scrambled one by one down to the pontoon for a leap ashore.

Now we had lots to talk about. Jenny's mother had foreseen this and said we must all stay for dinner. There were no refusals. Pete regaled us with some yarns about wartime life at Goose Bay and then we laid our plans for a water and land approach to the submarine next Saturday, when Ben could be our guide, though he admitted the route would be new to him, and probably rough going, when we left the river below the Falls and took to the woods.

Mrs. Matthews offered one piece of advice for which we were later most grateful. "Take lots of insect repellent," she said, "the black flies will attack you by the millions as soon as you leave the river. When I was young, my father made his own repellent from olive oil and Stockholm tar."

"Stockholm tar is new to me," said Karl.

"You'd know it if you ever owned a planked boat," replied Mrs. Matthews. "We pour the Stockholm tar over frayed or shredded hemp to make what all sea-going people refer to as oakum, which is used with a special chisel to caulk the seams between a boat's planks. Then, when the boat is launched into the water, the planks swell or 'plim' against the oakum and the boat can become as watertight as a bottle. Mixed with olive oil, however, and rubbed over the face and neck and hands, the tar can make your hide about four shades darker, especially when you've been in the sun for a while, and it takes a good many washings to get back to your real complexion; but it kept most flies away. You'll have newer repellents, of course, and be sure to take plenty. People have literally gone mad from black fly bites."

It was past ten o'clock, but still not nearly dark when we broke up and bid thanks and good night to Jenny and her mother. We had most plans made and the starting time was set for 6:00 a.m. on Saturday.

"Ralph," said Pete to me on the way back to his place, "this whole thing is nothing short of astonishing. Think of what the crew of that one submarine could have done if they had carried out their mission to disrupt the base. I am certainly looking forward to learning more from that Werner fellow. I hope Karl lets us know the minute he receives his father's letter."

Karl did. The letter arrived on Wednesday, and Karl telephoned at once.

8

Goose Bay at Risk

Karl brought the letter to Pete's place at dinnertime that evening, and Frank taxied up from the valley. Ben and Jenny had a party date with some friends. Pete had created an excellent stew and we tackled it with man-sized appetites. Pete's neighbour had contributed a pie made with red berries, which in Newfoundland I knew as partridgeberries.

Many Labrador people filled a barrel with them in picking season, and they could freeze and thaw through the winter without losing their tart tastiness.

The letter was a long one. Karl had already digested every detail of it. Here in brief is what he repeated to us.

Werner Holtz, as far as Karl's father knew, was the second of only two surviving members of Commander Ernest Runsted's U-boat crew. You will remember that Karl's father and grandmother had learned quite a bit from one man who had gone in the stolen motorboat to a coast rendezvous with another sub. He was subsequently the only survivor when the sub was destroyed by depth charges from one of our Canso aircraft.

Now Werner had spoken up. At age 40 he was recovering in 1965 from the loss of a kidney, and his wife had persuaded him to record his wartime experiences for their two children. The writing brought him unexpected peace and he decided he could now tell all he knew to Karl's father, who was certainly eager to hear it.

Normally a Class VII-C U-boat carried a crew of thirty-eight to forty-four men, but trained men were in desperately short supply by 1944 and, on this special mission, with orders to attack only targets which were almost undefended, they left port with a complement of only eighteen men. Werner was barely 19 years old and most of the others were 20 or younger. By 1944, after horrendous losses of U-boats and crews in the Atlantic, it was nothing unusual for men as young as 21 years to become commanders. Ernest Runsted, still commanding in his 40s, was an exception. A good officer, he knew the war was lost, and he considered further slaughter senseless. Almost a father to his crew, he wanted to save them not only from an underwater death, but also from the guilty conscience of killings which would have been just short of murder. Even a loyal and patriotic military man shuns war crimes.

He had already saved the life of a young crewman who was discovered senseless in a battery room near the keel when recharging under water. There was a snorkel to the surface to bring in air. In a heavy sea, the snorkel valve closed several times and fumes like chlorine rendered the young man unconscious. The commander brought him out, but at great cost to his own lungs, and his cough worsened for the rest of the voyage.

The trip through Lake Melville and up the Hamilton River has already been recounted, and also the escape of fourteen men in a large boat stolen from near Mud Lake. Three men stayed with the commander—Werner Holtz, Lothar Weiss and Willi Klus.

Normally, life in a submarine is unbelievably crowded, with practically no privacy. Ordinary crew sleep forward over the torpedo storage area, but sometimes half the sleeping space is taken up with stored food slung in hammocks or from pipes. The Wardroom and Officers' Mess forward of amidships and the Petty Officers' Mess just aft become mere passages when engine-room personnel change shifts or take over some additional combat duties.

On many missions of six weeks or even more, some crewmembers never see the sun, the sky, or even the sea. The two small loading hatches for torpedoes and galley being secured at the beginning of the voyage, and the bridge being accessible only to personnel on watch through the conning tower on surface runs, the atmosphere is often filthy, as are the men, with few opportunities to wash or change their clothes.

A whole submarine for only four people, with adequate food supplies for months and all the fresh water the river provided was a veritable paradise. The theft of a carton of food from Dew Drop Inn was merely a prank to prove to themselves that they could surprise the enemy if necessary, just as they could have taken over the whole weather station and direction-finding crew on Brig Harbour Island on their way to Hamilton Inlet.

In fact, they had emptied two brass shell cases from deck-gun ammunition and had buried them behind Dew Drop Inn on the transmitter site so that, if captured, they could prove their non-aggressive intentions.

"I'll look for those shell cases tomorrow," said Pete, "if there is no fire fighting practice on the concrete slab where the inn once sat."

One man always stayed on watch at the beached U-boat when the other three went exploring, often using an abandoned canoe which they had found and repaired. They had reported their position ("We know that," I said, "approximately latitude 53, longitude 61, the inland submarine which the direction-finding crews wrote off as an error"), and then awaited instructions which never came after the order to ship out all but four of the crew.

Broadcasts from the flotilla headquarters in France were regularly heard, but they contained only bombastic propaganda and challenges to the crews still operational to inflict mortal wounds on the enemy. They gathered nothing of the real course of the war from home transmissions, but learned everything from the radio of the men at Dew Drop Inn, behind which one or two men often crouched at night with Commander Runsted until his worsening cough threatened to betray him.

They had witnessed two aircraft crashes; one crew was altogether beyond help, but they dragged one man still alive from the second wreck. "And well I know it," said Frank. "I thank God for a compassionate enemy."

Posing in nondescript clothes as government surveyors, with the Commander doing all the talking, they actually gave some food to trappers and hunters who had run out of rations.

Finally, in the first week of October, with the Commander's health failing, he asked for a volunteer to break out somehow to the St. Lawrence River to contact a sub which could take news of their survival back to their families in Germany. It was a frail hope, but Werner volunteered. He got to Montreal as a stowaway on a freighter which had unloaded supplies for Goose Air Base at the Terrington Basin dock where security precautions seemed almost casual.

Werner had no Canadian identity and very little command of either French or English, so he lived as a vagrant, shuttling between

Montreal and Quebec City, with no possible way of contacting a U-boat, until the war was over.

Then he gave himself up and was repatriated to Germany with other prisoners, returning to Canada as a perfectly legal immigrant in 1950.

He never knew the fate of Commander Runsted nor of his crewmates Lothar and Willi.

"So," I said, when Karl finished his narration, "I have the solution to my mystery of the U-boat in the middle of coastal Labrador, but I'd like to stick with you, Karl, till we know your grandfather's fate. Frank will undoubtedly want to know what finally happened, and I bet Pete would like to know more of the man who could have destroyed him in his Dew Drop Inn bunk, and chose not to."

Karl was understandably emotional, though not to the point of tears. "I can hardly wait till Saturday," he said, "but I know we need Ben and Jenny to guide us to the sub. I'm really not much of a woodsman myself."

"I wonder what we will find," I said, and the same question was obviously on everybody's mind as we bid one another good night.

9

Karl on the Bridge

Pete and I were at the riverbank early on Saturday. We saw the sun come up and, as it gave its own colour to the quietly moving water for a few brief minutes, Pete said, "Arm of gold, *le bras d'or.* It's been said that such a sight as we see now, probably on a narrow inlet along the coast, inspired some poetic seaman in Jacques Cartier's ship to give the land its name, Labrador. Of course," he added, "there are other explanations."

We saw Jenny approaching, happily talking with Frank who accompanied her. "That young lady will never need to take the basin," said Pete. He saw the question in my glance and continued: "It's a superstition I don't fully understand because some women are reluctant to talk about it and others have different interpretations. However, it seems that on a certain night, maybe at New Year, if a young woman closes her eyes, has a basin of water placed in front of her, and then opens her eyes to look in the basin at the very moment of midnight, she will see on the surface of the water the face of the man she will marry."

"I think," I said, "that Jenny and Ben will settle that question with heart and head and not by superstition." Pete agreed.

Karl and Ben showed up together in Karl's car with the tools we thought we would need. Our food was in a couple of backpacks and we had all brought light waterproofs in case of morning dampness in the woods.

There's not much chance for conversation when a outboard motor monopolizes one's hearing, but that just makes the eye livelier and, on this glorious morning, I saw the river and its crowding evergreens as almost primeval, as though we were the first ones to see it. Man had so far left very few marks here. All was tranquil and it would have seemed an offence that a submarine, whose very purpose was death, should have passed this way if we had not known that there was no murder in the hearts and minds of its crew.

We were probably within hours of learning that U-boat's last secrets, and I'm sure that for all of us the anticipation was tinged with apprehension concerning what we might find— if we could enter a metal shell which had been sealed for twenty years. After all, three men were still unaccounted for.

We cruised within sight of the Muskrat Falls and could both see and feel the mist it created. We touched the edge of the turbulence, saw a log turn on end and disappear in the whirlpool, and tried without success to catch from river-level a glimpse of the telltale toppled trees that marked the sub's last resting-place.

So we retreated a mile or so downstream, found a good place to beach the boat and prepared for a hike through woods which gave no hint that any human had ever walked through them before. The sun was getting higher and the black flies knew it. We were grateful that, thanks to Jenny's mother, we were armed with repellent; however, those flies were of the kamikaze variety and swooped in suicidally despite our invisible shield. True, they bit less, but a surprising number of them got into mouth, eyes, ears, and nose. We quickly learned to endure and almost to ignore, except for our involuntary swiping when hands were free.

Ben and Jenny accepted the dense bush philosophically and moved more nimbly than the rest of us over the fallen trees. I was amazed at the depth of the moss due, of course, to the humidity created by the mist from the Falls. The fragrance of the evergreens was a delight and it was good to be alive.

In a small clearing, we made a fire— deliberately smoky to keep some flies at bay— and had a early lunch that was enjoyable for being more meditative than boisterous, before pressing on again.

Ben's sense of direction was perfect, especially in view of the endless detours around obstacles and, some time before noon, we stood breathless, more with excitement than from exertion, in a narrow inlet like a deep trench, alongside the low-lying, rusted, but intact hull of the war's last U-boat. Trees that were mature when her quiet electric motors drove her in there had toppled. Trees that were mere seedlings were now tall enough to take over the responsibility of concealing from any passing view all that was not hidden by the crew's original camouflage.

The conning tower leaned slightly towards the river; it was obvious that the swirling waters in the large pool under the Falls were eroding the spit of sand and trees between the hull and the river. Eventually the submarine would topple and, given time, if its hatches were left open to permit flooding, it would disappear under the whirlpool.

There were a few quiet moments, almost indecisive. "Let's not move too many trees," I said. "We'll need the concealment for a while yet, and we can certainly get on the bridge with a bit of scrambling. You should be first, Karl."

"Only on the bridge, not below," he replied, and we watched as he climbed up and stood quietly facing forward over the chest-high screen where his grandfather had often stood with streaming oilskins, and with the wind and sea in his face. We saw him caress the railing, examine the periscope stubs and the gun mountings, and down he came.

"I didn't try the hatch," he said almost apologetically. "If the sub is a tomb for anybody inside, the hatch will probably be secured from below and we won't get in. I'd rather somebody else tackled the hatch first."

Pete, Ben and I were given the nod by the others and, climbing up with two crowbars, we pried with a will. Despite hinges that were almost welded with rust, we managed with some straining to lift the hatch. There was a collective sigh, more felt than heard, as six people resumed breathing.

We hadn't given much thought to the state of the air inside, but it was not in the least offensive, and it was obvious that the ventilation ports had been left open. We lit two Coleman lanterns and checked our flashlight before Ben descended the ladder, closely followed by Pete and myself.

I had been in a British submarine briefly in the course of my wartime duties and I had inspected a German VII-C U-boat after its 1945 surrender, so I knew what to expect as far as the crowded but efficient layout was concerned.

In the present case, first of all, we were relieved to see that our apprehensions were groundless, for there were no remains of human bodies. There was quite a lot of rust due to condensation, and the multitude of battery cases in both compartments had split due to freezing, though there was little acid damage since, when batteries are fully discharged through use or age, most of the sulphate is in the plates rather than in the liquid electrolyte.

Almost everything that could decompose or mildew had been disposed of, as had the torpedoes and ammunition. There were no flags. All was shipshape and in good order, evidence of proper discipline to the very last.

On the table in the small compartment which served as the commander's cabin, there was something which I knew would be of supreme interest, but we decided to let Karl handle it first.

Ben was at ease below decks and filled with active interest. Pete felt a bit uncomfortable, so he and I climbed up and out while Karl, Frank and Jenny scrambled up the bridge and below to join Ben.

The black flies must have found better meat elsewhere, so, as we sat on our waterproofs enjoying the sun, Pete said, "I had an odd feeling down there. It was not really claustrophobia, but more as if I was in the presence of jannies."

"Aren't jannies just what we in Newfoundland refer to as mummers?" I asked.

"To some Labrador people they are," Pete answered, "but others think the disguised visitor might be inhabited by the returned spirit of someone who has departed this life. As we worked our way aft through those small passage openings in the bulkheads to see the diesels and the electric motors, I half expected some silent figure in a working uniform to beckon us closer."

He continued, "I had somewhat the same feeling when I heard Frank tell about his rescue from the crash by people unexpected. I'm sure Charlie Crowley when he beached his boat, saw Frank's splint, and then saw the man who called to him from the edge of the woods, was wondering if he had seen a pre-season version of Old Smoker."

Pete answered my question before I asked it. "You're wondering who Old Smoker is. Plenty of older hunters or trappers, lost in a blizzard with a dog-team, will tell you that Old Smoker guided them home. He is a ghostly figure, muffled in winter gear, who is dimly seen through the storm beckoning the lost man onward to safety, and always managing effortlessly to keep ahead. You'd have to get the whole story from a real trapper and I can point you to one man, lost on his way to a rendezvous with a friend in a remote cabin, whose earlier snow blindness was aggravated in a blizzard by stinging snow in his eyes. Up until the moment his eyes failed him completely, he had been following Old Smoker, dimly seen. Though he could no longer lift his eyelids, his tired dogs picked up enthusiasm and ran eagerly forward until they suddenly stopped. He groped his way blindly along the dogs' traces to give the leader a kick, and tripped over the step of the cabin he was looking for. Don't ever take Old Smoker lightly," Pete finished with unexpected seriousness.

We lay back, enjoying a profound sense of well-being, and surveyed a cloudless sky over tall trees until the others came tumbling up the ladder onto the bridge and down to the ground. Karl was carrying the bundle which I had seen on the commander's table and had asked him to retrieve.

It was obviously the U-Boat's logbook, wrapped in cloth and in multiple layers of oiled paper. Karl handled it as a rare treasure, slowly unwrapping the coverings. Inside, in addition to the book, was a bar of six medals complete with ribbons. We all crowded in eagerly for a first look at the logbook; there was a note in English on a neat sheet of paper inside the front cover:

> To the finder of this log. Would you please do me the great kindness of sending this log, when peace returns, to my wife and son whose names and address are listed under Next-of-Kin on the log's first page. I am sorry I shall have no way of thanking you.
>
> Signed, Commander Ernest M. Runsted.

Frank was visibly moved as he said, "For my part, I need no greater thanks than the kindness he showed me when he tied his scarf around my splints."

The records in the log itself were in German. "Let's go home now," said Karl, and when we cut the motor and pulled the boat ashore at Happy Valley he promised, as we turned to go our separate ways, that he would work on the translation at once and would let us know the book's contents as soon as he could.

10

Stop; Finished with Engines

Only Frank and I could meet with Karl in his neat apartment the next afternoon. He had slept a mere four hours the previous night, had skimmed through the early part of the logbook which told essentially what we already knew, and had concentrated on the last few pages. The revelations were sad and interesting.

In his own hand, the commander told of his failing health and increased difficulty in breathing. He told of Werner's successful boarding of the freighter in his bid to reach the St. Lawrence, but had no knowledge of the outcome.

He recorded repeated attempts on the part of Lothar and Willi to have him surrender to any airman or officer on the air base so as to get medical help, but he knew he was beyond it.

The last entry he wrote was on October 13, 1944. He suffered little pain but was too weak to leave the sub. He had suggested that Lothar and Willi should abandon him to his fate and try to escape south, as Werner had done, before the navigation season ended. He reported their respectful refusal with obvious pride and admiration. His last words were a wistful expression of love for his wife and son, and the hope that they would understand that his turning away from war at the last was neither treason nor cowardice but a reluctance to inflict any further suffering or death in a cause that was already lost, and about whose basic principles he now had serious doubts.

"Above all," he finished, "I fervently pray for peace in a world where my country can hold its head high, not by reason of military superiority, but because of achievements in science, culture and compassionate human relations which will truly enrich mankind."

His hand had hardly faltered to the last, but he had written no more.

Willi finished the log, and his entries set Karl his final task. There was no entry for October 14 but on October 15 the log read: "Commander Ernest Runsted died at 1045 hours this day. Lothar Weiss and the writer Willi Klus have vowed to give fitting burial to a man whose courage in the face of danger was never in doubt, whose concern for those who served under him brought out the best in every man, and whose compassion embraced any helpless enemy as well as his suffering companions-in-arms."

Then came the part that left us something to do. After the crash of Frank's plane, the four Germans, moving around the perimeter of the base cautiously but freely, witnessed the funeral of one of the aircraft's crew in the small base cemetery. They were determined that the commander would not have a lonely grave in the wilderness near Muskrat Falls, but that he would lie in the company of other honourable fighting men.

They laid him out in his dress uniform, sewed his body in blankets as for a burial at sea, but took him downstream in the abandoned canoe they had repaired for use, and patiently carried him on a improvised stretcher through the woods to the cemetery, about five miles from the river.

There, undisturbed, they dug a grave a short distance from the existing ones so that it would not be encroached upon too soon, and laid his body to rest, burying with him, before the grave was fully filled in, the U-boat's sextant and the smaller of its two compasses. They decided to leave his medals with the logbook.

Willi's last entry, dated October 17, stated that they would now attempt to escape to Montreal by the route that Werner had taken, though the only way they could even guess that he had eluded capture was the fact that their hiding-place had never been betrayed.

Only an examination of records of ship departures from Terrington Basin on that approximate date would reveal on what ship or ships they might have stowed away. We have no way of knowing what finally happened to them though we might find out yet, if this account is ever published.

The part which was of supreme interest to Karl, and which would enable him to complete his quest, was the careful description of the grave's location. At that stage of the war, most of the burials in the cemetery were identified by a wooden cross or a temporary wooden marker, which might not have been permanent. However, a few military headstones, so familiar to those of us who have visited Flanders, were already in place. Lothar and Willi had chosen two of these as reference points, recording their inscriptions in full and then indicating the distance and compass direction from each. The point at which the lines crossed would mark the commander's grave. Of special interest was their symbolic choice of distance, reflecting the last position of the submarine recorded in the log. They had paced out 53 strides from one stone and 61 from the other.

Karl consulted us anxiously. "Do you think we could soon have a look at the grave site without arousing too much curiosity?"

"I'm sure we can," was my reply. "I have friends buried there and in my visits I've never met another person. But first, let's find some cord and a couple of pegs."

Karl looked puzzled, so I explained. "Willi gave us directions in numbers of strides. We can do things much more easily with stretched cords pegged at the end nearer the headstones. A stride when you are measuring distance usually averages 33 inches, so let's do the arithmetic and reduce strides to feet and inches."

We did so; 50 strides became approximately 146 feet and 61 strides came close to 168 feet. With a twelve-foot carpenter's tape, we measured out the proper lengths from a ball of sturdy wrapping twine and then set out in Karl's car.

From Karl's apartment in the Department of Transport section of the base, it takes only a few minutes to get to the cemetery. We quickly located the two substantial headstones mentioned in the log, guessed at the compass directions which were hardly necessary anyhow, since there was only one point at which the two lines would intersect if their length was measured from the front of the stones, set our pegs and stretched the cords.

We arrived a point which was probably outside the bounds of the cemetery proper, which Frank felt was a mark of sensitivity on the part of Lothar and Willi since they had no way of knowing how Canadians would react to having an enemy buried in ground reserved for their own war dead and for base civilians who died during their tour of duty.

"It wouldn't matter now," I said. "I have been at the War Museum in Canberra, the capital of Australia, and the pieces of two miniature Japanese submarines are on display. They were dredged up from Sydney Harbour following their distruction in World War II after sinking one ship and damaging others. The remains of four Japanese crewmen were found in the subs, and even during the war they were given honorable military funerals. When peace came their ashes were returned to Japan, and family members were invited to Sydney to drop wreathes over the places where the submarines had been destroyed. War is an atrocity which can only make us wonder when we will come to our senses. Karl's grandfather saw that long before most others in uniform."

Frank had not said much all day, but he spoke up now. "I believe," he said, "that Karl wants to dig deep enough to find the sextant and compass. We'll have to go away anyhow for a shovel or two, so why not come back here when Pete and Ben and Jenny can join us. There will be lots of light after we've had dinner."

That sounded like good sense and fair play. Ben got off work at five o'clock and Pete's shift ended at four. Two telephone calls from Karl's place sealed the plan, and by a few minutes after six o'clock, having eaten more quickly than was good for our digestion, we met at the point we had marked as the grave site. Excitement and anticipation showed in all of us, but they made Jenny's bright face even livelier and lovelier.

With two steel rods which Ben had brought, we probed the surface soil which was light and sandy at that point. Willi and Lothar had measured well and within five minutes one of the rods hit an obstruction.

Dignity and decency kept us from any loud demonstration and we spoke almost in whispers as Pete and Frank took the shovels and began to dig. Two feet down they found two well-wrapped objects; the two crewmen had once again made good use of oiled paper from some rust-protected machinery.

Karl did the unwrapping in a silence which was unplanned and reverent; if we had been wearing hats we would have bared our heads, but they were already bare. The compass, in a brass mounting of course, was barely discoloured. The wooden case which held the sextant showed some marks of dampness, but the sextant itself was as clean as when the navigator last held it.

If this were a movie script with an over extended budget, the story might stop right here, with six people gathered round the grave of the courageous though perhaps controversial man whose story would have lacked a last chapter if his grandson had not embarked on a determined search.

But there are a few things yet to be said. Of the six, Frank was the only one to have seen the commander and that was through a haze of pain. He now took the scarf which he had kept for twenty-one years and gave it to Karl, neatly folded and with the initials *EMR* uppermost. A few words were spoken between them and a firm handshake exchanged as Karl in return gave Frank the compass. Beckoning Karl a short distance from the rest of us, Frank exchanged with him a few more words which we did not try to hear. Karl nodded as he came back to replace the sextant in its case and wrappings, and then allowed Pete to help him bury it again.

Then we left, with subdued good-byes. Later that evening, Pete produced two brass shell cases. "I spoke to the American Base Commander," he said, "and got permission to dig behind the wartime site of the Canadian Dew Drop Inn. The shells were there, just as Werner Holtz told Karl's father. The six of us in our bunks had no idea that we were separated from an armed enemy by only the thickness of a wooden wall. Frank is not the only Canadian to owe his life to Ernest Runsted."

"Does Karl know you found these?" I asked. "He does," said Pete, "and he said that you and I could have them as mementos if we chose." Mine is on my desk as I write, brightly polished as always.

Back in Toronto via Montreal three days later, my cheerful wife and two lively daughters heard the details I could not always give in my telephone calls from Labrador. Frank called me about a week later, suggesting that our wives and children meet, and we invited them for dinner the next day. His son and my daughters met easily, as teenagers usually do, and our wives were instant friends.

While the others were talking elsewhere, Frank and I were in my sunroom study. He unwrapped a heavy parcel about the size of a large book and showed me a slab of polished granite which read, in neatly chiselled letters:

In Memory of
U-Boat Commander
Ernest Martin Runsted
1901-1944
A True Hero
By Sparing Life He Gave Life

"I wanted to provide this," he said, "because in the cemetery I saw one grave on which the marker said 'Eskimo Not Known' and it gave me a sensation of unutterable sadness. I've met Karl's parents, and they have approved of the wording on this stone. They may apply to the government to have the bounds of the cemetery enlarged to include the commander's grave. In the meantime, as I suggested to Karl at the graveside, this slab will replace the sextant under the surface. Perhaps the two coordinates of 53 strides by 61 form a wholly appropriate way of identifying the grave's location if they decide on no other action.

"That will depend on the Commander's widow, still living, who will be coming to Toronto and then to Goose Bay with Mr. and Mrs. Runsted where Karl will meet them. The United Church minister in Happy Valley, himself a veteran RCAF officer at Goose Bay during the war, has agreed without reservation to meet them quietly at the grave for a private funeral. I think, all told, we did well."

I agreed.

Karl's grandmother, we learned later, chose not to see the submarine, nor to display it to others. Ben, Jenny and Karl visited it several more times until the progressive leaning made boarding it too dangerous. By the time the ice went out of the river the next spring, the U-boat had toppled and slid under the water.

All the friendships formed during these adventures have lasted and deepened, so I end with one last note. Five years after the events recorded here, Jenny and Ben came to Toronto on their honeymoon. She was still full of life and lovelier than ever, and he was even prouder than before of her smiling, wholly natural grace. Their future is full of rich promise, as is the future of Labrador if we recognize and encourage the fine qualities that so many of its young people display.